CAREERS ON THE FRONT LINE

ARMY CAREERS

SARAH EASON

CRABTREE
PUBLISHING COMPANY
WWW.CRABTREEBOOKS.COM

CRABTREE
PUBLISHING COMPANY
WWW.CRABTREEBOOKS.COM

Author: Sarah Eason
Editors: Jennifer Sanderson
Ellen Rodger
Proofreader: Tracey Kelly
Indexer: Tracey Kelly
Editorial director:
Kathy Middleton
Interior design: Emma DeBanks
Cover and logo design:
Katherine Berti
Photo research: Rachel Blount
Print coordinator:
Katherine Berti
Consultant: David Hawksett

Written, developed, and produced for Crabtree Publishing by Calcium Creative Ltd.

Photo Credits:
t=Top, tr=Top Right, tl=Top Left
Inside: Joint Base San Antonio: p. 15; Jose E. Rodriguez: pp. 1, 24; U.S. Air Force: Senior Airman Brett Clashman: p. 21; Senior Airman Clayton Cupit: p. 3; Raymond McCoy: p. 23; U.S. Army: p. 11; Staff Sgt. S. Patrick McCollum: p. 25; Steve Stover: p. 20; U.S. Army National Guard: Maj. Joseph Siemandel: p. 17; U.S. Northern Command: U.S. Air Force photo by Tech. Sgt. Efren Lopez: p. 8; U.S. Department of Defense: Army Spc. Geoffrey Cooper: p. 29; Air Force Master Sgt. Matt Hecht: p. 6; Army Sgt. Alon Humphrey: p. 28b; Army Sgt. Thomas Mort: p. 28t; Navy Petty Officer 3rd Class Danny Ray Nuñez Jr.: p. 7; Wikimedia Commons: p. 12; Tech. Sgt. Brian Boisvert: p. 27; Jonathan Mallard: p. 9; Sgt Paul Robbins: p. 16; Robert on Flickr: p. 5; Staff Photographer: p. 19; U.S. Army photo by staff Sgt. Kyle Davis: p. 4; Spec. 5 Vince E. Warner: p 13. Front cover: Shutterstock

Library and Archives Canada Cataloguing in Publication

Title: Army careers / Sarah Eason.
Names: Eason, Sarah, author.
Description: Series statement: Careers on the front line | Includes bibliographical references and index.
Identifiers: Canadiana (print) 20200283855 | Canadiana (ebook) 20200283863 | ISBN 9780778781387 (hardcover) | ISBN 9780778781448 (softcover) | ISBN 9781427125781 (HTML)
Subjects: LCSH: United States. Army—Vocational guidance—Juvenile literature. | LCSH: United States. Army—Recruiting, enlistment, etc.—Juvenile literature. | LCSH: Canada. Canadian Army—Vocational guidance—Juvenile literature. | LCSH: Canada. Canadian Army—Recruiting, enlistment, etc.—Juvenile literature.
Classification: LCC UB147 .E27 2020 | DDC j355.0023—dc23

Library of Congress Cataloging-in-Publication Data

Names: Eason, Sarah, author.
Title: Army careers / Sarah Eason.
Description: New York : Crabtree Publishing Company, [2021] | Series: Careers on the front line | Includes index.
Identifiers: LCCN 2020029752 (print) | LCCN 2020029753 (ebook) | ISBN 9780778781387 (hardcover) | ISBN 9780778781448 (paperback) | ISBN 9781427125781 (ebook)
Subjects: LCSH: United States. Army--Vocational guidance--Juvenile literature. | United States. Army--Juvenile literature.
Classification: LCC UB323 .E27 2021 (print) | LCC UB323 (ebook) | DDC 355.0023--dc23
LC record available at https://lccn.loc.gov/2020029752
LC ebook record available at https://lccn.loc.gov/2020029753

Crabtree Publishing Company
www.crabtreebooks.com 1-800-387-7650

Printed in the U.S.A./082020/CG20200710

Published in Canada
Crabtree Publishing
616 Welland Ave.
St. Catharines, Ontario
L2M 5V6

Published in the United States
Crabtree Publishing
347 Fifth Ave
Suite 1402-145
New York, NY 10016

Published in the United Kingdom
Crabtree Publishing
Maritime House
Basin Road North, Hove
BN41 1WR

Published in Australia
Crabtree Publishing
3 Charles Street
Coburg North
VIC, 3058

CONTENTS

PROTECT AND DEFEND

An army is a part of the military, which is the armed forces that protect a country. Soldiers in an army are trained to protect their country and the people who live in it from enemy attack. They also protect the interests of that country, such as property and citizens who live overseas. This may involve fighting in battles, but it also includes peacekeeping and **security** missions. Most armies work alongside several other military units, including the navy and air force. When an army needs to move about, it often uses these units' aircraft and watercraft.

TOUGH GOING

People who train to be soldiers in the army have to be prepared to act and think quickly in dangerous and stressful situations. Troops are groups of soldiers. They might be sent to fight an enemy in scorching hot mountainous deserts or thick, muddy forests. Soldiers may be separated from family and loved ones for many months at a time. All soldiers have to be physically and mentally tough to survive in these difficult situations.

Frontline soldiers are soldiers in the army who have the most contact with an enemy, such as during hand-to-hand fighting.

CALL TO ARMS

On September 11, 2001, an extremist **terrorist** group named al-Qaeda attacked the World Trade Center in New York City and the Pentagon in Washington, as well as several commercial aircraft. The Trade Center's Twin Towers were destroyed, and nearly 3,000 people were killed. Al-Qaeda leaders were believed to be based in Afghanistan. The United States and its **allies** sent forces to Afghanistan to destroy al-Qaeda and its leaders and to ensure the safety of people in the United States and around the world.

After the al-Qaeda attack on the Twin Towers, Army Reserve soldiers were called in to help the injured and to organize rescue and recovery operations.

Your FRONTLINE Career

Look for "Your Frontline Career" boxes. They highlight the skills and strengths needed for specific Army careers. They can be used to help you decide whether a career in the Army is for you and what roles might suit you best.

FRONTLINE CAREER CHOICES

An army consists of several units. In the United States, this includes the standing Army of professional soldiers, which is involved in active service, the Army Reserve, and the Army National Guard. Canada also has both a standing Army and reserve soldiers. Reserve soldiers serve part-time and work regular jobs the rest of the time.

RESERVE SOLDIERS

In some armies, reserve soldiers may train other soldiers or be required to work a set number of weeks each year in the Army. To keep up high levels of fitness, reserve soldiers have to commit to regular training sessions. Reserve soldiers provide backup during emergencies or unexpected situations, usually at home. These situations may include natural disasters, such as floods or wildfires. The National Guard in the United States is a group of soldiers, each of whom serves for eight years. Each U.S. state also has its own National Guard.

Soldiers take part in tough exercise routines every day.

Army doctors often carry out general health checks on civilians, or ordinary people, in countries in which they are stationed. They also treat soldiers injured during battles.

BEHIND THE SCENES

Being part of the Army is not all about fighting. Once basic training is over, there are many different specialist roles a soldier can train for. Even though some of these jobs do not involve combat, they are essential to the safety and well-being of military **personnel** and the success of fighting missions. Noncombat soldiers (those who do not fight), such as medical doctors, look after soldiers and their families at military bases. Many armies have soldiers based around the world. They live in special bases with their families. While they are in the army, they are provided with medical care and other services, such as housing and education for children.

ARMY VALUES

Army training prepares soldiers to fight under difficult circumstances, but it also teaches them life values. Loyalty and duty to their country and each other is important. Respect for other people, other **cultures**, and self-respect means that soldiers are taught to appreciate what other people do and also to recognize their own work. Integrity, or doing what is right and honest, is important to help develop trust and respect. Having personal courage means being able to face individual fears and standing up for personal beliefs.

TRAINING FOR THE JOB

Soldiers can then go on to train in other areas of the armed forces, depending on their skills and abilities. For example, they could choose training in technology, science, engineering, law, music, or cooking. They can then work in their chosen field for the army.

FRONTLINE FOOT SOLDIERS

Infantry soldiers are sometimes known as foot soldiers. They mainly fight on foot, rather than in trucks or tanks, and are usually the first to be sent into battle. Infantry soldiers are trained to fight in hand-to-hand combat in freezing mountain conditions or sweltering rain forests. They are also trained to use a wide range of weapons, including rifles, hand grenades, and anti-tank weapons.

TRACKS AND TRAPS

Fighting overseas in enemy territory means that infantry soldiers are at a dangerous disadvantage. The enemy is likely to know the land where the battle is being fought very well, and they will have knowledge of the best hiding places and sites for surprise attacks. Infantry soldiers need to be experts in map reading and **navigation**, so that they can track the enemy without falling into a trap or getting lost, especially at night. They also need training in **minefield** safety, constructing barriers such as trenches and roadblocks, and knowledge of how to operate and maintain army equipment, such as radios.

Infantry soldiers have to be prepared to fight in extreme weather conditions, such as freezing temperatures and deep snow.

Soldiers who work with specialized weapons are called artillery soldiers. Here, artillery soldiers are using a ***howitzer*** *during a combat mission in Afghanistan.*

HEAVY GUNS

Artillery soldiers are soldiers who are trained to use high-powered weapons to support units fighting on the front line. They protect infantry and tank units, as well as land and sea territory, from enemy attack. Their weapons include howitzers and launchers that fire shells, rockets, and missiles at the enemy. Their mission is to destroy enemy weapons and buildings, and to protect against air and sea attacks.

A CREW OF FOUR

Usually, each artillery crew is made up of about four soldiers who are responsible for one weapon. Each soldier in the unit has a specific task, such as to position the gun, load it, aim the gun at the enemy target, and fire the gun.

Foot Soldier Stories

William Swenson:

HERO ON THE GROUND

In 2009, U.S. Infantry Army Captain William Swenson was in Afghanistan. He was there to teach the Afghan Border Police how they could set up better and safer borders. On September 8, Swenson set off with 100 troops and border police to Ganjgal, a small village in the hills northeast of Kabul, the capital of Afghanistan. The Ganjgal villagers had asked for help from the military to restore their damaged mosque, and Swenson's team had been sent to assist them.

Swenson knew that the request from the villagers could be a trap. There were many **Taliban rebels** in the area near the village, and it was possible that the rebels were behind the request for help. This is a well-known enemy **tactic**. When Swenson and his men walked into the village, enemy fire suddenly came from all sides. As he had feared, they had walked into a trap. Swenson and his team dived for cover, but many of the soldiers were hit and injured.

Swenson and two other soldiers rushed to help a comrade, or soldier on the same side, who had been wounded. They tried to stop the soldier's bleeding and called for air support—all the time under constant fire. When Swenson spotted an enemy gunman creeping toward him and the wounded soldier, he hurled a grenade at him—saving himself and his comrade from being shot.

Your FRONTLINE Career

Is Being a Foot Soldier for You?

Sounds Great

- Daily fitness training will get you in shape
- Travel and being posted anywhere in the world, from Africa to Afghanistan or Europe
- Working as part of a team

Things to Think About

- Being posted far away from home, family, and friends for long periods of time
- Following rules and taking orders from those more senior than you are

Swenson called for help, and an armed attack helicopter quickly responded to his call. As the helicopter fired on the village, the Taliban rebels began to run away. Swenson and other unwounded soldiers helped their seriously wounded comrades into the helicopter. Swenson then **commandeered** a nearby pickup truck and drove back to collect the remaining wounded men, until they were all rescued.

Meanwhile, nearby, the Taliban had attacked and killed a team of **Marines** and dumped their bodies in a trench. Swenson and his team took control of an army truck and drove to the trench through enemy fire. They were helped by **scout helicopters** circling above, looking for the enemy. While one soldier fired a machine gun at the rebels, Swenson and the others carried the bodies of their fallen comrades to the truck.

In 2013, Captain Swenson was awarded the Medal of Honor for bravery.

Captain William Swenson (pictured above right) put his own life on the line to save the lives of his fellow soldiers.

ARMORED DIVISION

When soldiers go into combat, they are often accompanied by armored units. These are groups of soldiers who fight using tanks and other heavy vehicles armed with powerful weapons. Soldiers in the armored units complete advanced soldier training after basic training. This includes how to use heavily armed fighting vehicles. They also learn **reconnaissance** skills and how to gather and send information back to army **commanders**. The role of these soldiers is essential in supporting infantry. Armored units often lead infantry into combat, so the soldiers have some protection against enemy fire.

IN THE TANKS

Armored tanks can fire at an enemy that is more than several miles away. They can also move quickly over rough ground. Tank crews are responsible for driving and maintaining all tanks, loading and firing a tank's main gun and machine guns, and making sure that a tank's communication equipment works properly. It is hot and cramped inside armored tanks. Despite this, during fighting, soldiers are trained to wear full army uniform, including a helmet, at all times.

Tanks can provide the long-range heavy weapons necessary to support soldiers in the world's worst combat areas.

INTO THE UNKNOWN

Infantry usually fight in unknown territory. They often do not have any idea of what or who is ahead, or which way to go, especially at night. Under these conditions, without the help of a reconnaissance team, foot soldiers are walking blindly into the unknown. Reconnaissance vehicles are equipped to survey, or study, the landscape far beyond human sight, night and day. They send back information to the commander, who can then decide on a plan of action. If the vehicles are unable to travel across an area, the crew will carry out the reconnaissance on foot, using whatever equipment they can carry with them.

DIFFERENT TANKS

*There are many different types of tanks. The U.S. Army's Abrams tank provides maximum firepower against heavily armored enemies. Some versions are also built to survive **nuclear**, **biological**, and chemical attack. The fast Stryker is lighter than a tank. It can carry people and equipment to combat zones.*

The Canadian Cougar is an armored reconnaissance vehicle that can travel across both land and water.

ARMORED Stories

Ezra Maes: SURVIVING DISASTER

In 2018, a freak accident in a 65-ton (59 metric ton) Abrams tank caused gun loader Ezra Maes to lose his leg. Maes and two other crew members were in Poland, in Eastern Europe, as part of a U.S. mission to assist allies in ensuring borders were secure from the Russian Army. On the second day of a week-long exercise, the crew were asleep in their tank when they were suddenly jolted awake. The huge machine started rolling downhill and was quickly speeding up.

Your FRONTLINE Career

Is Being in an Armored Unit for You?

Sounds Great

- Learning how to maintain tanks and work the guns
- Being part of a tight-knit team
- Travel to many different countries

Things to Think About

- Spending time confined to small spaces, because you will be cooped up in the tanks for long periods of time
- Frontline fighting is dangerous
- Being away from home a lot

Maes called to the driver to stop the tank, but the brakes failed, so it was impossible to make an emergency stop. The soldiers realized they were in danger but could do nothing—they just held on to whatever they could inside the tank. Eventually, the tank crashed into a mud wall at the bottom of a steep canyon. All the crew were badly shaken and injured. The gunner (a soldier who uses a gun), Aechere Crump, had cut her leg and it was bleeding heavily. She also had a broken arm. The driver, Victor Alamo, was trapped in the driver's area with a broken back.

Maes's badly crushed leg was caught in a **turret gear**. He had also broken his **pelvis**, ankle, and shoulder. Maes pulled at his leg to free it, so he could get to the medical kit to help his crew. As he did so, he felt a tear, and his leg came away. Maes began to bleed, and the heavy loss of blood made him dizzy. He was going into shock. However, Maes's army training helped him keep calm. With quick thinking, he undid his belt and used it as a **tourniquet** to stop the bleeding.

Ezra Maes had to learn to walk again at the Brooke Army Medical Center using a prosthetic leg. He believes he is lucky to be alive.

The crew realized that the tank's radio was broken, and no one knew where the soldiers were. They also realized that if they didn't get help soon, they were all likely to die. Then, unexpectedly, Maes's phone buzzed—it was still working. Despite the pain he was in, he managed to unlock the phone and send a message asking for help to a friend.

All three of the crew were found and rescued by the Army. Maes spent four months in intensive care. He had months of rehabilitation therapy, which is special care and treatment. With determination and toughness, Maes recovered from his injuries and learned how to walk again with a **prosthetic** leg. Maes used this experience to follow a new career path. Today, he works as a prosthetist, helping others who have lost limbs while on assignment.

ARMY INTELLIGENCE

Armies need information to help them plan military operations. Military intelligence is a unit that collects the information needed by army commanders. The information may include things such as the terrain or weather conditions where soldiers are fighting or the position of enemy soldiers. The information is analyzed, assessed, and passed on to commanders, who use it to make important decisions about their fighting plans.

GATHER AND ANALYZE

Intelligence is crucial in helping keep soldiers safe and making sure combat attacks are successful. Intelligence operators are people who gather information on the enemy. They work mainly in offices at bases around the country. They may also work on board ships or other vessels at sea or be positioned overseas. Sometimes they may work with the Army, Air Force, Navy, or Special Operations Forces (SOF).

Intelligence operators are trained to use high-tech computers and equipment. They have to judge and analyze vast amounts of often incomplete and confusing data, or information. This then has to be turned into reports that can be sent to commanders. Sometimes timing is essential to saving lives of soldiers fighting on the front line, so intelligence operators must think and act quickly. Training helps them build the confidence they need to make swift decisions in stressful circumstances.

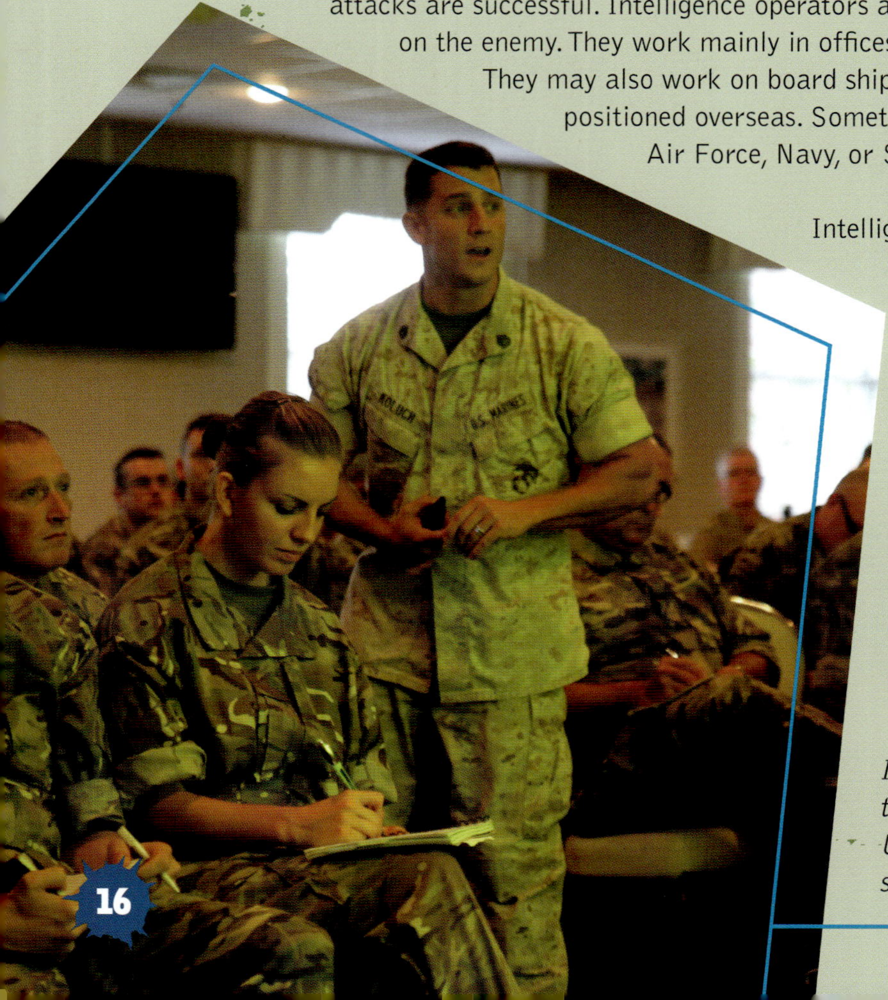

Intelligence officers often work together with other forces. Here, a U.S. intelligence officer briefs British soldiers on a top secret mission.

UNDER PRESSURE

Intelligence operators need to be able to work under pressure, make quick and often lifesaving decisions, and be prepared to take responsibility for those decisions. They have to be self-disciplined and confident. In most armies there are many different intelligence roles that a person can be trained for. The skills a person learns as an intelligence officer can be developed into a career in business management, as a private investigator, security consultant, ***paralegal****, or* ***intelligence analyst****.*

Intelligence specialists learn foreign languages, so that in an emergency, they can communicate with different people in their own languages.

KEEPING SECRETS

Much of the information intelligence works with is highly classified, or top secret. If it falls into the wrong hands, it could be a threat to soldiers' lives. Intelligence operators must make sure that they keep highly classified material safe and secret—even from family and friends.

INTELLIGENCE Stories

Mary Legere: SPY TRAINER

Mary Legere joined the U.S. Army in 1982. She was commissioned through the Reserve Army officers' training program and joined Military Intelligence. She took a number of training and education courses, including master's degrees at the U.S. Army War College—one in military science and one in military strategy.

Legere's first job was as a leader of a small military unit in West Germany for three years. She then took her Military Officer Advanced course and was sent to the Republic of Korea (South Korea) and Iraq. In 2004, Legere was based in the Republic of Korea where she was responsible for trying out new high-tech software to gather and analyze intelligence. This technology helped speed up the time it took to analyze information and create reports. This would help save the lives of soldiers on the front line.

Legere loved the excitement of her job and felt she was making a real difference. With hard work and determination, along with her ability to analyze facts and data, think on her feet, make quick decisions under pressure, stay calm, and inspire those around her, she worked her way up the Army ranks.

When she was based in Baghdad, the capital of Iraq, Legere was responsible for the planning, coordination, and success of intelligence and **counterintelligence** operations. Her role as Deputy Chief of Staff for Intelligence of the Multi-National Force—Iraq (MNF–I) was to oversee the collection of intelligence, analyze it, and make sure it was sent to the soldiers on the front line.

Your FRONTLINE Career

Is Being in Intelligence for You?

Sounds Great

- Spending your days coding, computer programming, and problem-solving
- Working with the latest world-class technology
- Using your decision-making skills and analysis of facts to protect frontline soldiers

Things to Think About

- Spending most of the time in an office and not on the front line
- Focusing and being able to concentrate for long periods of time without being distracted
- Having to make decisions under intense pressure

Mary Legere received the Saint Isidore Army Cyber Award for her leadership skills and intelligence knowledge, which helped the fight against terrorism.

As Director of Intelligence for U.S.-led forces, Brigadier General Legere started a program to train Iraqi women to become spies. To help win the fight against terrorists in Iraq, local women were **recruited** to take the Basic Military Intelligence Course. They were trained to provide U.S. commanders with valuable local information.

In 2012, Legere was made Lieutenant General and became the Deputy Chief of Staff for Intelligence of the United States Army. She had become one of the most powerful people in U.S. Intelligence, and she led the way for more women to take top positions in the intelligence services.

CYBERWAR

Digital technology is becoming increasingly important to national and military security. To make sure they can keep their soldiers, intelligence, and countries safe, armies have developed cyberwarriors. These are people who fight from a desk, not in the field. Cyberwarriors are trained to defend computer and information systems or to attack enemy systems.

PANIC AND CONFUSION

Cyberwar is when one country attacks another country's digital systems, using computer viruses, **malware**, and other Internet threats. Computer systems that control airports, trains, traffic lights, electrical power grids, hospitals, and banking systems may be knocked out. This can cause widespread panic and confusion, and it can seriously affect the security of the country. Malware can also be used to disrupt nuclear programs.

Cyber Mission Force (CMF) teams are part of U.S. Army Cyber Command, a special unit set up to protect U.S. cyberspace from attack from terrorists and other national and international threats.

CYBERWARRIORS

Many countries, including the United States and Canada, are now giving top-level cyberwarrior training in cyberdefense and cyberattack. Being a cyberwarrior involves working with top secret, highly sensitive information. Skills that will be developed include software development systems that can predict incoming threats and how to identify and analyze malware. Cyberwarriors work with all areas of the military, including the air force and navy. They keep an eye not just on overseas enemies, but also on threats from within the country, such as threats from terrorists or computer hackers.

The U.S. Army Cyber Command has operators and analysts that specialize in using cutting-edge technology to perform cyberspace operations.

BECOMING A CYBERWARRIOR

Cyberwarriors can be recruited from anywhere, including civilians who have the right experience. Cyberwarriors must be skilled in digital technology and math. They need strong analytical skills and must be able to work under pressure and respond quickly. They must also be prepared to constantly develop their knowledge and work well by themselves or as part of a team. Cybersecurity is one of the fastest-growing job sectors. With their training and experience, cyberwarriors can go into many different areas. These include being a software engineer, data scientist, senior cybersecurity operations expert, and radio frequency engineer.

CYBER Stories

National Security Agency:

FIGHTING ISIS

The U.S. Army Cyber Command is a crack team of military cyberwarriors. Military personnel work with civilians to improve their skills in tracking and hacking, or getting into, enemy social media, such as Twitter, YouTube, and Facebook. The aim of the military is to develop ways that the Internet can be used to hack into enemy accounts. When it does this, it can gather information about how the enemy works and track its movements. The military can also use the Internet to attack an enemy's media operations by causing confusion, spreading rumors, and bringing down enemy media systems.

In 2016, Cyber Command and the National Security Agency (NSA) launched Operation Glowing Symphony. The people in this secret task force had a special mission to hack into the Islamic State of Iraq and Syria (ISIS) and bring down its media operation. ISIS is an Islamic terrorist group that wants to establish strict Islamic rule in parts of the Middle East. For ISIS, the Internet is crucial to its ongoing operations and success. It needs the Internet to recruit new followers from around the world, to spread **propaganda**, move money around, and communicate.

The cyberteam discovered that ISIS used ten social media accounts to control all its media operations. The team hacked into the ISIS accounts using **phishing** emails, so that it could gain control of the accounts. It then put **spyware** and malware onto computer **servers** so it could set itself up as account administrators. As administrators, the team could access ISIS emails and information.

Your FRONTLINE Career

Is Being in the Cyber Command for You?

Sounds Great

- Working on computers and in particular on social media
- Using detection skills to figure out how the enemy is working
- Being creative to stay one step ahead of the enemy
- Working on your own and being part of a team, too

Things to Think About

- Working long hours in an office
- Patience to collect and sift through masses of data and paperwork
- Not much frontline action

Cyber Command personnel take courses to increase their knowledge of computer science to make sure they are always one step ahead of the enemy.

Then the battle really began. The cyberteam created small problems on the ISIS websites. These included changing passwords, slowing downloads, deleting content, putting photos where they should not be in videos, and draining cell phone batteries. All this was designed to confuse and frustrate ISIS, especially since the actions seemed like human error or everyday problems rather than a targeted attack.

ISIS also lost accounts as the cyberteam made sure servers went down. Although ISIS has a lot of cash, it does not have the credit cards or bank accounts to buy new servers and **domain addresses**. As a result of the attack, ISIS was unable to produce its online magazine, and many of its foreign language websites disappeared afterward.

MEDICAL CORPS

The Army Medical Corps is made up of surgeons, nurses, dentists, and other specialized medical workers who care for soldiers and their families. Single soldiers often live in barracks with other soldiers, while married soldiers live on an Army base or nearby. All soldiers have access to medical care at doctor's practices, hospitals, and dental and medical clinics.

ON THE BATTLEFIELD

Army doctors must ensure that soldiers are fit enough to fight before they are sent to combat zones. Soldiers who are injured while fighting and who need medical help right away are rushed to field hospitals. These are small, mobile medical units that can be put up close to where the fighting is taking place. These tents have lifesaving equipment, and Army surgeons and nurses work night and day caring for the injured. Medical teams on the battlefield often have to work in terrible and dangerous conditions. They need to think and act quickly to save soldiers' lives.

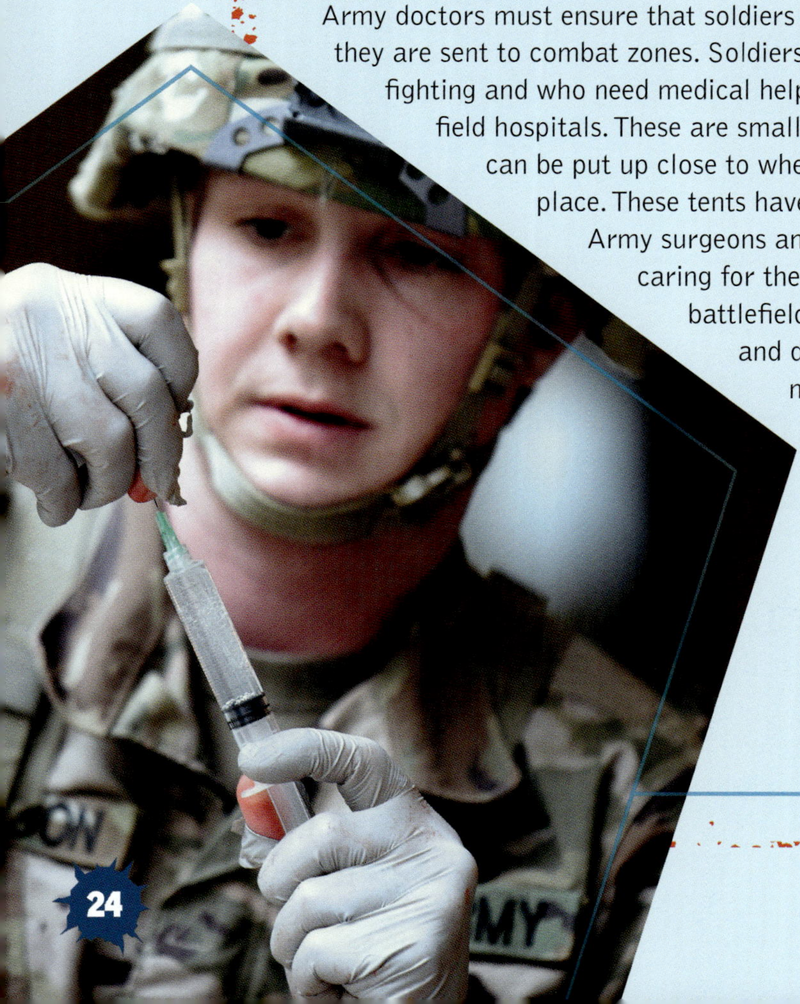

Army combat medics are soldiers trained to carry out first aid and emergency medical treatments on the battlefield.

DISASTER!

Natural disasters, such as floods, wildfires, landslides, tornadoes, and tsunamis, can affect thousands of people. These events can leave whole areas without food and water, and they can make people homeless. Hundreds of people may be injured and need emergency medical help as a result of these disasters. Most armies are trained to provide **humanitarian** missions that rescue people from danger and provide emergency medical help. They can also deliver **vaccinations** against diseases.

This Canadian medical camp in Haiti was set up by the Army to save lives and help those who are injured.

TRAINED TO HELP

In some armies, medical personnel do not have to do the basic army training program. Instead, they take an officer training course. This teaches basic soldier and leadership skills, army values, and how the medical unit works. Officers who complete either officer or basic training can then go on to complete their medical training or have more training in specialist roles, such as a ***physical therapist*** *or* ***laboratory technician****.*

MEDIC Stories

Alannah Gilmore: SAVING A FRIEND

Alannah Gilmore served in the Canadian Army as a medic, providing first aid and emergency care to soldiers wounded on the front line. In 2007, she was based in Afghanistan. One night, she was called to attend to a soldier who had stepped on a landmine (a type of bomb) outside a small village a long way from help. He was alive but had lost a foot. His other foot was badly damaged by shrapnel, which is small, sharp pieces of metal. The soldier was in enemy territory and possibly surrounded by terrorists. Alannah had to get him out—and quickly.

Your FRONTLINE Career

Is Being a Combat Medic for You?

Sounds Great

- Caring for people, whether they are your own soldiers or local people living in the area of conflict
- Working under extreme pressure on the battlefield

Things to Think About

- Seeing a lot of blood, broken bones, and seriously injured people
- Being away from home for long periods of time
- Being prepared to protect yourself from the enemy

Alannah grabbed her medical kit, pistol, and rifle and raced to the armored Bison ambulance. When she reached the soldier, Jody Mitic, he was in pain and covered in mud. Jody was a sniper in the Army—a sniper is a person who shoots at targets from a long distance away. That night, Jody had been leading his team to check out a village. The team members were wearing night-vision goggles so they could see what was ahead in the dark, but Jody could not see the landmine that lay buried in the ground.

As Alannah gave Jody emergency treatment, she remained alert to what was going on around her. She was in enemy territory, and there was a strong possibility that she could be attacked at any time. Although Alannah knew that her responsibility was to get the patient to safety, she was also aware that she needed to keep safe herself, too. If she had to shoot the enemy to protect herself and her patient, she would.

Night-vision goggles are essential for soldiers fighting in enemy territory in the darkness of night.

Other soldiers helped Alannah carry Jody on a stretcher to the ambulance. When the blood and mud was removed from Jody's face, and with the light from the ambulance, Alannah was shocked to discover that the injured man was her close Army friend. She had been sitting with him only the night before, relaxing before the mission the next day. Working quickly, Alannah managed to get Jody to the helicopter collection spot, where he was airlifted to the hospital and treated for his injuries. Jodie survived, but he lost both legs just below the knee.

In a happy ending, Alannah caught up with Jody in Canada when her Army service overseas ended. Their friendship grew and eventually blossomed into love. They are now married with a family.

COULD YOU BE ON THE FRONT LINE?

Do you have what it takes to be a frontline soldier? Here are some of the key things to think about if you want to join the Army.

EDUCATION

To get into the U.S. Army as an infantry soldier, you need a high school diploma or GED. For the Canadian Army, you need to complete Grade 10 or Secondary IV in Quebec. Being a good student and enjoying learning means that you have a better chance of success in the Army training programs.

FAMILY

When you join, the Army recruiter may want to talk to you and your parents. Explain to your parents why you feel it is important to join the Army, so they understand why you want to enlist.

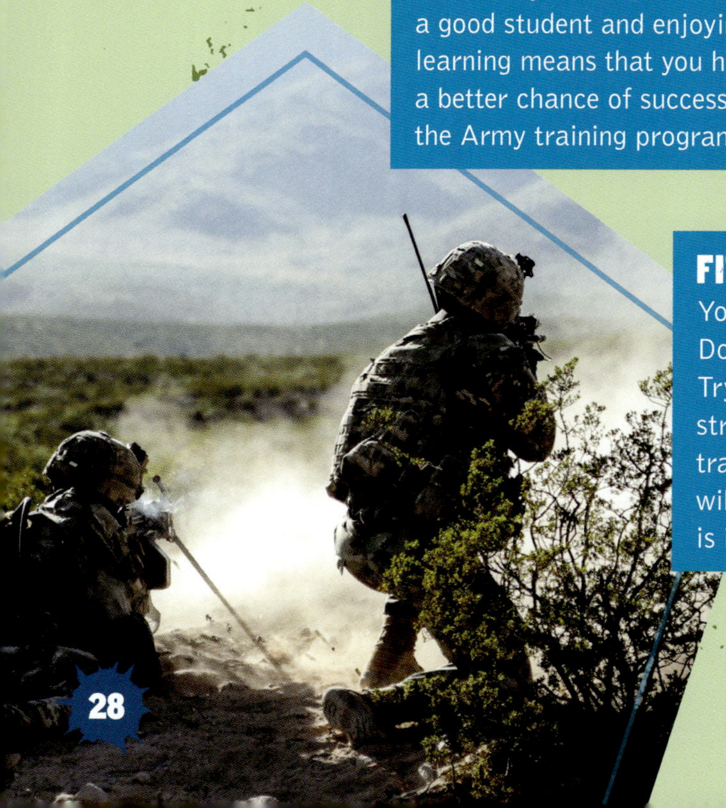

FITNESS

You need to be fit and healthy to join the Army. Do plenty of exercise and eat a healthy diet. Try different types of exercise to improve your strength and stamina, such as running, weight training, and swimming. Playing team sports will help you build team skills, something that is important in the Army.

DISCIPLINE

The Army has high standards of discipline. It expects soldiers to follow orders, keep their beds and uniform neat at all times, and have their weapons ready for action. Learn to keep your room and clothes clean and tidy. Keep your schoolwork organized.

COMMITMENT

Training for the Army is tough. The days are long. You need commitment to be able to keep going when you are mentally and physically exhausted. When you have the opportunity, say "yes" to challenges in your everyday life that will stretch you physically and mentally, especially fitness challenges.

THE FUTURE

The Canadian and U.S. Armies have many different training programs. Think about what you would like to specialize in as you progress through the Army.

VALUES

Think about how you treat your family and friends and how you behave. The Army looks for people who are honest, loyal, hardworking, brave, and respectful.

LEARN MORE

To find out more about life in the Army and what it offers, go online (see links on page 31), or contact a local Army recruiter. A recruiter will be able to answer all your questions.

GLOSSARY

active service Being in battle
allies Countries or groups that agree to work together
biological Describes germ warfare, which is a system of using deadly bacteria and viruses to attack people
commandeered Took possession of
commanders Senior military officers who are responsible for directing soldiers and making decisions
commissioned Appointed or assigned
counterintelligence Keeping the enemy from discovering military or government secrets
culture The religion, art, and way of life of a people or country
domain addresses Names of websites
hand grenades Small explosives that are thrown by hand at the enemy and explode when they land
howitzer Large gun that fires shells
humanitarian Describes the action of caring about the welfare and happiness of people
intelligence analyst A person who reads, understands, and explains secret information gathered by the intelligence or spy service
laboratory technician Someone who works with scientific equipment, usually performing experiments
malware Computer software that damages and disrupts computers, and allows others to gain access to computers illegally
Marines Soldiers trained to fight on land and sea
military intelligence Secret information gained by the armed forces, usually about the enemy
minefield A place where explosive devices are buried
navigation To find one's way from one place to another, especially in unknown areas
nuclear Describes weapons that use deadly and destructive nuclear energy
paralegal A person trained in legal matters but who is not a fully qualified lawyer
pelvis The large bone at the base of the spine and between the hips
personnel The people who work for an organization or company
phishing Illegal online communications that pretend to be genuine to persuade a person to give personal information, such as a password
physical therapist A medical person trained to help people with physical injuries or disabilities
propaganda Information spread to promote a particular cause
prosthetic Describes an artificial body part, such as an artificial leg
reconnaissance To secretly find out about enemy territory
recruited Encouraged to join an organization by someone within the organization
scout helicopters Helicopters used to help infantry by guiding them or tracking them in enemy territory
security Protection against an enemy danger or threat
servers Computers or devices that hold a lot of information that they can pass to other computers and devices
spyware Software used to secretly gain access to a computer, so it can spy on the user's activities and steal secret information
tactic A plan or way to achieve a specific goal
Taliban rebels Illegal fighters who belong to a violent religious group that wants to rule in Afghanistan
terrorist A person who uses illegal fighting and violence for political or religious gains
tourniquet A device, such as a belt or strip of cloth, used to keep blood from flowing out of a wound
turret gear The handle used to turn the gun in the turret, on top of a tank
vaccinations Injections to prevent diseases

LEARNING MORE

Discover more about the Army and careers on the front line.

BOOKS

Boutland, Craig. *Attack Vehicles on Land: Tanks and Armored Fighting Vehicles* (Military Machines in the War on Terrorism). Capstone Press, 2019.

David, Jack. *United States Army* (Torque Armed Forces). Torque Books, 2015.

Russo, Kristin J. *Surprising Facts About Being an Army Soldier* (What You Didn't Know About the U.S. Military Life). Capstone Press, 2017.

When I Grow Up I Want To Be ... in the U.S. Army! Jake Learns about the U.S. Army. Wigu Publishing, 2014.

Peppas, Lynn. *Tanks at War.* Crabtree Publishing, 2016.

WEBSITES

Learn more about the roles of U.S. Army officers at:
www.army.mil/ranks

The Army Reserve Officers' Training Corps (AROTC) has a scholarship program for chosen enlisted soldiers to train and become officers. Learn more about it at:
www.goarmy.com/careers-and-jobs/current-and-prior-service/advance-your-career/green-to-gold/pocket-scholarship.html

Find out more about joining the Canadian Armed Forces at:
https://forces.ca/en/how-to-join/#btt

To learn more about how to join the Canadian Infantry, visit:
https://forces.ca/en/careers

The Canadian Army offers specialist training programs for Indigenous peoples. Find out more at:
https://forces.ca/en/programs-for-indigenous-peoples/#cfaept

INDEX

ABOUT THE AUTHOR

Sarah Eason has written books on many different subjects, from geography and history to science and art. In researching this book, she has learned about both the challenges and rewards of having a career on the front line, and how those in service make a positive contribution to the lives of people all over the world.